This book belongs to:

For my mother —E.B.

For Mom, for letting me play outside —C.G.

 Published in the United States by Schwartz & Wade Books, an imprint of Random House Children's Books, a division of Random House LLC, a Penguin Random House Company, New York.

Schwartz & Wade Books and the colophon are trademarks of Random House LLC.
Visit us on the Web! randomhousekids.com

Educators and librarians, for a variety of teaching tools, visit us at RHTeachersLibrarians.com

Library of Congress Cataloging-in-Publication Data
Bram, Elizabeth.
Rufus the writer / by Elizabeth Bram ; illustrated by Chuck Groenink. — First edition. pages cm.
Summary: Rather than a lemonade stand, Rufus sets up a story stand one summer and makes a series of trades with his friends—a story for a shell, for a kitten, for a surprise, and one more as a special birthday gift for his sister.
ISBN 978-0-385-37853-6 (hc) — ISBN 978-0-385-37854-3 (glb) — ISBN 978-0-385-37855-0 (ebk)
[1. Creative writing—Fiction. 2. Barter—Fiction.] I. Groenink, Chuck, illustrator. II. Title.
PZ7.B7357Ruf 2015 [E]—dc23 2014010945

The text of this book is set in Aaux Pro.
The illustrations were rendered in gouache, acrylics, pencils, and Adobe Photoshop.
MANUFACTURED IN CHINA
2 4 6 8 10 9 7 5 3 1
First Edition

RUFUS the writer

by
Elizabeth Bram
illustrated by
Chuck Groenink

schwartz & wade books · new york

Rufus was watching a cloud shaped like a cushion turn into a cat when the idea first came to him. "I'm not going to have a lemonade stand this summer," he said. "I'm going to have a story stand!"

Then he ran into the house to gather pencils and paper and markers.

STORIE

Soon Millie and Walter came by. “Do you like our outfits?” said Millie. “We decided to wear only our favorite colors.”

“Cool,” said Rufus. “Do you like my story stand?”

“Awesome,” said Walter.

"Want to come swimming with us?" asked Millie.

"I can't," said Rufus. "I've got a story stand to run."

"Okay," said Walter. "I'll take one story, please. How much?"

"Just bring me a special shell from the beach," said Rufus.

After they left, Rufus wrote his first story.

Orange Is the Best Color

Red and Yellow
got married
and had a baby
named Orange.

When Orange got big and went to school,
he met lots of other colors.
Purple and Green became his best friends.
Orange was so popular, he got voted
Best Color by the other students.
And that is how we came to know
that Orange is
the best color.

Rufus was illustrating the story when Sandy walked up with a big box.
“Hey, Rufus,” he said. “Guess what? Rainbow had kittens!”
“Wow!” said Rufus. “I’ll trade you a story for that cute little black one.”
“You can have her for free,” said Sandy.

“Oh, she’s worth a lot more than that,” replied Rufus. “Come back later and I’ll have your story.”

Then Rufus began to write.

The Wallet and the Cat
One day Henry was walking home and
he saw a wallet lying on the sidewalk.
Since he collected old wallets, he
picked it up and looked inside.
Five million dollars fell out!

Henry took the wallet and the money to the police station, but nobody claimed it.
So he put the money in the bank.
Then he took out a million dollars and bought a kitten.
Henry named the kitten Misty.
And he never played with his wallet collection again.

While Rufus was illustrating his story, his little sister, Annie, brought out her tea set and began pouring tea for her dolls.

"Want to play tea party?" she asked.

"Sorry, Annie," said Rufus. "I'm busy working."

"Okay, maybe tomorrow," said Annie, "when it's my birthday."

Oh, right, Rufus remembered. And now he knew just what to give her.

This is Annie's birthday story:

Annie and the Dancing Teapot

Annie could not pour the tea because the teapot and the cups would not stop dancing. "I want to be a teapot, too!" she said.

Quick, quick, quick,

Annie jumped onto the table and shrank to the size of a teacup. She had fun talking to the teacups while they all danced.

But when it came time to pour the tea, Annie was too small to do it. She huffed and puffed until she was very thirsty.

Quick quick quick, Annie jumped off the table and became **BIG** again. Then she drank the tea all up.

Mmmmm!

Just as Rufus was illustrating his new story, Sara walked by.
"What are you doing?" she asked.
"I'm writing stories for my stand," said Rufus. "Would you like one?"
"Yes," Sara replied. "Can it be about buttons?"
"Sure," said Rufus.

"How much will it cost?"

"Whatever you think," said Rufus. "Surprise me."

"Okay," said Sara, and she ran off to figure out what to trade for Rufus's story.

This is the story Rufus wrote:

Buttons, Buttons, Buttons

Daddy is a button, and I'm a baby button.
We live in a house made of buttons –
big buttons, little buttons,
shiny buttons, button buttons.

We have a button tree and
a button cat. We eat off
button plates on
a button table.
We have buttons
on our buttons
and buttons on the buttons
on our buttons
and buttons on the buttons
on the buttons
on our
buttons.

The sun was sinking in the sky when Millie and Walter came by with Rufus's shell.

"I love it!" said Rufus as he put it to his ear.

Next Sandy came by and handed Rufus the little black kitten.
"I'm going to name her Misty," said Rufus, and handed Sandy his story.

Sara skipped over carrying a big bouquet of flowers. She gave it to Rufus in exchange for her story.

"These look just like your buttons," he said. "Thank you!"

ORI

While everybody was reading, Annie said, “I wish I had a story, too.”
“You do!” said Rufus. Then he gave her the early birthday present.
“This is my best present ever!” said Annie. “Can you read it to me?”
“Of course,” said Rufus.

And he did.

22

se the tea
d not stop da
be a

he Best Color

d and
ot married
nd had a baby
named Orange.